Arthur O'Shaughnessy

Arthur O'Shaughnessy, his Life and his Work

With Selections from his Poems

Arthur O'Shaughnessy

Arthur O'Shaughnessy, his Life and his Work
With Selections from his Poems

ISBN/EAN: 9783744722223

Printed in Europe, USA, Canada, Australia, Japan

Cover: Foto ©Raphael Reischuk / pixelio.de

More available books at **www.hansebooks.com**

ARTHUR O'SHAUGHNESSY HIS LIFE AND HIS WORK WITH SELECTIONS FROM HIS POEMS

BY

LOUISE CHANDLER MOULTON

MDCCCXCIV

CAMBRIDGE AND CHICAGO
Published by STONE & KIMBALL
LONDON: ELKIN MATHEWS & JOHN LANE

To the Memory of Five Friends

What wailing wind of Memory is this
    That blows across the Sea of Time to-day,
    Blending the fragrance of a long-dead May
With breath of Autumn — agony with bliss?

Philip Bourke Marston.

My thanks are due to Rev. A. W. Newport Deacon, the cousin and literary executor of Arthur O'Shaughnessy, and also to his publishers, Messrs. Chatto & Windus, for permission to use the selections included in this volume.

L. C. M.

March, 1894.

CONTENTS

	Page
INTRODUCTION	13

FROM AN EPIC OF WOMEN
AND OTHER POEMS:

Exile	49
The Cypress	52
A Whisper from the Grave	53
Bisclavaret	59
The Story of the King	68
The Fountain of Tears	72
There is an Earthly Glimmer in the Tomb	76

FROM LAYS OF FRANCE:

From the Lay of the Nightingale	79
From the Lay of Two Lovers	82
From Chaitivel	88
From the Lay of Eliduc	92

Contents

Page

FROM MUSIC AND MOONLIGHT:

Ode 99

Has Summer Come without the Rose ? 103

Three Gifts 105

Now I am on the Earth . . 106

A Dream 107

At the Last 108

FROM SONGS OF A WORKER:

At Her Grave 111

Lynmouth 113

A Love Symphony . . . 117

In a Bower 119

INTRODUCTION

Arthur O'Shaughnessy

HIS LIFE AND HIS WORK

" What voice is this?"

AMONG the poets of whom more ought to be known, any student of English poetry for the last twenty-five years would certainly class Arthur William Edgar O'Shaughnessy. None of his four volumes, published in London, has been reprinted in America; and they have, perhaps, been little read here save by certain poets and critics. Yet they contain much that poetry-loving readers can ill afford to miss. By virtue of his best work, O'Shaughnessy must always hold an honorable place in the roll of the Victorian poets. As his friend and brother poet, Edmund Gosse, said of him in the Academy, soon after his death, his work was of unequal merit, but when whatever is trivial in it has been winnowed away there must remain, as long as English verse is preserved, a residuum of exquisite poetry, full of odor and melody, and essentially unlike the work of any one else.

The facts of Arthur O'Shaughnessy's life are few. His career was in no wise eventful. He lived in his friendships, his loves, his griefs, and his work; and quiet years went by him, marked only by the ebb and flow of the tide of song. He was of Irish descent, but born in London, on the 14th of March, 1844. He was in some sense a protégé of the late Lord Lytton, who was an old friend of his mother, and was one of the first to discover and delight in the boy's genius. It was through Lord Lytton that he received an appointment, in 1861, as a junior assistant in the department of printed books in the British Museum, whence he was transferred, in 1863, to be a senior assistant in the Natural History Department. Here he remained until his death, passing the rest of his working days in the classification of fishes and reptiles, "in a queer little subterranean cell, strongly scented with spirits of wine, and with grim creatures pickled round him in rows on rows of gallipots."

He brought out his first volume of poems in 1870, and dedicated it to his friend, John Payne, who also published in that same year his own first volume of poems, and dedicated it to Arthur O'Shaughnessy. Soon after the appearance of these volumes, inscribed to each other, these two young poets began to be known in London literary society, and were frequent guests at the far-famed evenings of Ford Madox Browne, the artist, whose house was at that time a center of literary and artistic hospitality. Those delightful evenings in Fitzroy Square were given up after the death, in 1872, of the son of the house, that "marvellous boy," Oliver Madox Browne, poet, painter, and novelist, all in one. With the death of this only and idolized son, Mr. Ford Madox Browne withdrew for some time from society, and ceased to be the gay and debonair host, under whose roof choice spirits were wont to make merry; but while those famous evenings lasted what noctes ambrosianæ they had been! The old house to begin with—the

oldest and largest in solemn old Fitzroy Square
—was the very abode which Thackeray peopled
with his Newcomes. It was big enough for
a castle, and it had wide and lofty rooms, and
massive stone staircases, and long underground
passages leading to vaults which might have
served for dungeons; a house haunted by
echoes, and with winds whispering secrets in
its great chambers; cool in the hottest summer day, and in the winter needing all the
riotous warmth and brightness of the fires
which used to fill its old-fashioned fireplaces,
and roar up the wide-mouthed chimneys. And
what men and women came there in those
days! Some of them are ghosts now, and
haunt, mayhap, the old rooms still. Rossetti
was there, THE Rossetti, painter of poems, and
poet of pictures; his sister, Christina, who is
now so seldom seen outside her quiet home;
their brother, William Michael, the critic, who
afterward married a daughter of the Madox
Brownes. William Morris came, too—he who
divides his time, now, between writing poems
that will live, and planning decorations for
houses for other people to live in—and with
him came his wife, whose beauty he sang and

His Life and his Work

Rossetti painted, till she became part of the literary history of the Victorian epoch. She was "divinely tall," this "daughter of the gods," and by many accounted the most "divinely fair" woman of her time. She is a striking figure yet, with her remarkable height and her equally remarkable grace, her deep eyes, her heavy, dark hair, and her full, sensitive red lips. But in those old days she was young still, and in our picture—

> Give her back her youth again,
> Let her be as she was then!
> Let her have her proud, dark eyes,
> And her petulant, quick replies;
> Let her sweep her dazzling hand,
> With its gesture of command,
> And shake back her raven hair
> With the old, imperious air.

In another corner sat William Bell Scott. He—as well as Ford Madox Browne, himself—died not long ago, and even at the time of which I speak he was no longer young, except in the sense that with his sunny, gentle, childlike nature he must be young immortally. Like Rossetti, Scott was both poet and painter, and his work should, in justice to his genius, be far more widely known than it is. Dr. Hake was a frequent guest; and Swinburne; and Theodore Watts, poet and critic—but Watts belongs to the younger men.

The younger men were in great force at these Fitzroy Square symposia; and among them it would have been impossible not to notice O'Shaughnessy, with his handsome, sensitive, clearly cut face, his bright, earnest eyes, behind the glasses which gave him a student-like aspect, his rather slight but well-knit figure, with the noticeably small feet and hands, so well-shod and gloved, in which he took an innocent pride. He was full of enthusiasm, and I think, had length of days been given him, he would always have been the youngest man in every company. What pleasure he had in things small and great! He was as simply frank in his appreciation of his own work as in that of other people, and I shall never forget the quick "Like it, eh?" and the sudden light in his eyes when he perceived that something he was reading or reciting had found its way to his listener's interest. He was half a Frenchman in his love for and mastery of the

His Life and his Work

French language; and many of his closest affiliations were with the younger school of French poets. He used to pass most of his vacations in Paris, where he always received the warmest of welcomes. He was one of Victor Hugo's most ardent admirers, and his visits to "the master," as he was wont to call Hugo, were among his memorable delights. But he delighted in everything. A kind word, a child's shy caress, a bit of smoky London sky with a red sun struggling through it, the sigh of the wind, the sea breaking against a stretch of ragged coast, the beauty of a woman, the handclasp of a man, books, pictures, music, the drama—how he loved them all! I think sometimes that, with his keenly enjoying nature, he compressed more happiness into his thirty-six years of life than most men, even men of imagination, find in a life that lasts on into hoary age.

He was full of interest even in his "specimens" at the museum—his butterflies, his lizards, his serpents. He had come, before his death, really to be recognized as an authority on reptilia.

I never saw him dull. Some little thing had always interested him, and I half wondered

the mummied insects with which he was sur-
rounded did not quicken into life under the
magnetism of his so living touch. And yet
there must have been a melancholy side to
this sunny nature, for through his poetry there
thrills forever a minor chord. Perhaps he
walked in the sunshine with his friends, and
went alone into the shadow. I shall speak
later of the haunting and prophetic sadness of
some even of his earliest work. But first let
me follow the course of his too brief life to its
sudden end.

An Epic of Women, 1870, was a remarkable first volume and it had a remarkable suc-
cess, which at once gave its author a decided
position among the poets of his time; and, from
him who had done so much already, people
expected much more. In 1872 he published
his Lays of France, and in 1873 he married
the eldest daughter of Dr. Westland Marston,
the dramatist, and sister to Philip Bourke
Marston, the poet. Mrs. O'Shaughnessy was
a person of rare mental gifts. She was at once
imaginative and witty. In conjunction with
her husband she published a volume of sto-
ries for children, entitled Toy-Land. But,

charming as this work was, her share in it very inadequately represented her varied gifts, which only the ill-health following upon the births and deaths of her two children prevented her from using for the public.

It seemed as if, for the small group of people of whom O'Shaughnessy was one, misfortune began with the death of Oliver Madox Browne. It was followed by the loss of the O'Shaughnessy infants; by the death of Mrs. O'Shaughnessy's only sister in 1878, and by Mrs. O'Shaughnessy's own death in the February of 1879. The grief of our poet at this last supreme loss was such as belongs to the poetic temperament—not deeper or more sincere than that of other men, but certainly more picturesque. He told those who knew him best how he was haunted by his wife's presence; how constantly she dwelt in his thoughts; how impossible it would be to forget her. And yet his was a poet's nature, and must needs have been consoled. It is not, I think, the men of imagination who grieve forever, but rather the practical men, who find no outlet for their sorrow in beautiful words, and have no fancy with which to bedeck the image of some consoling angel. In the very nature of things Arthur O'Shaughnessy must have loved again—had begun to do so, in fact. In this second summer of the heart, all his wonderful capacity for happiness would surely have reasserted itself; but just then, as if his dead wife reached pale hands from under the earth to draw him toward her, in one week from the time he went out gaily to witness the performance of a favorite actor he lay dead, with a woman's idle tears falling upon his unresponsive face. He died on the 30th of January, 1881, a week less than two years after the death of his wife. As his brother-in-law, Marston, wrote, on the anniversary of his death :

> Thou wert so full of song and strength and life,
>   Hadst such keen pleasure in small things and great,
>   It hardly can seem real to know thy state
> Is with the ancient dead.

I think all of us who knew him felt something of what these lines express. He had been so keenly alive, it did not seem possible that he could be dead. Instinctively one turned, in the old haunts, to speak to him—even as so often we spoke of him. Who knows that he did not hear ? Only that voice—that flexible, sweet, clear voice of his — answers us no more, and it is the first time he was ever unresponsive to a friend. So much for his "fair, fleet, singing life," as Marston called it in the poem from which I have already quoted. It remains to speak of his work.

I have said that his first volume, An Epic of Women, was a very remarkable book. It contains some poems which he scarcely surpassed afterward for rhythmic beauty and originality of conception. Also it was noticeable for a strange vein of poetic sadness, and the more noticeable because the man himself was so gay and riant. It may be that in secret his soul foreboded, even then, the brief life and sudden death that awaited him. It would almost seem so, from one of his saddest and most pathetic poems, A Whisper from the Grave.

The title of An Epic of Women is, perhaps, scarcely justified by the contents. In the part of the volume specially included under this head, we find first that audacious, mystical, sensuous, Swinburnian poem, Creation. Mr. Gosse says of this poem that, "As some Catholic writers have been drawn through mysticism into sensuousness, O'Shaughnessy

Arthur O'Shaughnessy

was led through sensuous reverie into mystical exaltation. His much maligned and misrepresented poem, Creation, is, if we exclude the cynicism of the last stanza, pure Catholic doctrine, and might have been signed by St. Bernard." This poem is followed by The Wife of Hephæstus, Cleopatra, The Daughter of Herodias, Helen, and A Troth for Eternity. Read this superb word-picture of the Serpent of Old Nile, with which the Cleopatra opens:

> She made a feast for great Marc Antony:
>   Her galley was arrayed in gold and light;
> That evening in the purple sea and sky,
>   It shone green-golden like a chrysolite.
>
> She was reclined upon a Tyrian couch
>   Of crimson wools; out of her loosened vest
> Set on one shoulder with a serpent brooch
>   Fell one white arm and half her foam-white
>   breast.
>
> And with the breath of many a fanning plume,
>   That wonder of her hair that was like wine —
> Of mingled fires and purples that consume —
>   Moved all its mystery of threads most fine,
>
> And under saffron canopies all bright
>   With clash of lights, e'en to the amber prow
> Crept, like enchantments subtle, passing sight,
>   Fragrance, and siren-music soft and slow.

His Life and his Work

In Helen, and more notably still in A Troth for Eternity, we discern a fine dramatic quality, which the strong lyric bent of Mr. O'Shaughnessy's genius has somewhat obscured in the larger part of his work. Helen is represented as weary at last of Troy, and going back in memory to the old days in Greece, and longing, woman-like, for what she had carelessly thrown away. A Troth for Eternity suggests memories of Rossetti, and also of Browning, without containing anything that could distinctly be traced to either. The revelation in it of the man's unconscious madness, through his conscious and jealous love, is given with a subtlety and strength, surprising indeed when regarded as the work of a young man of twenty-five. The Fountain of Tears is a poem of such pure and perfect beauty, one can hardly praise it too strongly. O'Shaughnessy seldom wrote sonnets, and still more seldom was at his best in them; but he has given us one in this volume that we could ill afford to miss: "There is an earthly glimmer in the tomb!"

In this volume, also, we find Bisclavaret, of which Mr. Gosse speaks as the "reverse of

the medal " from such poems as The Fountain
of Tears, the sonnet just mentioned, Chaitivel,
and others. In the whole, however, of this
brilliant, interesting, but unequal first book
there is certainly no more original poem than
Bisclavaret. Its motif is drawn from the le-
gends of the Were-Wolf, and so faithfully does
it picture the inhuman ecstasies and savage fire
and passion of

> The splendid fearful herds that stray
>   By midnight, when tempestuous moons
> Light them to many a shadowy prey,
>   And earth beneath the thunder swoons,

that the reader shudders with a vague and
nameless fear, as if one were, perforce, a spec-
tator of these unholy raids. The poet's imagination revels in the presentment of lonely
places, given up to wild winds and spectral
moonlights ; and his sympathy with the law-
less lives of these evil phantoms, with their
keen relish of the night and of pursuit, their
cruelty aching like hunger, and their mad glee
over the fallen, is so perfect, one half believes
that all of this he saw and part of it he was.

One merit of this volume is its simplicity of

purpose—and by this I do not mean simplicity of idea or of method, but that simplicity which came of absolute loyalty to his own conception and ideal. No man loved the appreciation of his fellows better than O'Shaughnessy. He basked in praise, as a flower in the sunshine; but he never made a bid for it by the slightest sacrifice of his own conception of the rights and purposes of art, at least in either of the books published during his lifetime. From some of his posthumous poems it may be inferred that he either departed from his former lines because he had gone beyond them, or else he was seeking for his Muse a more solid ground than her wayward feet had hitherto possessed. I should be guilty of an unpardonable omission, did I fail to mention, in connection with An Epic of Women, the fantastic but most interesting drawings with which his friend, John Nettleship, enriched it. Since those days Mr. Nettleship has become famous as a painter of animals. In the Grosvenor gallery of 1883 one of the most moving pictures was his Blind Lion; helpless forest-king, whom now even the jackals dared to flout.

Mr. O'Shaughnessy's next volume was Lays

of France, a collection of metrical romances, loosely founded on the Lais of Marie de France. This book contains some of the most divinely lovely lyrics which O'Shaughnessy ever gave to the world, and in one of the Lays, namely Chaitivel, I am inclined to think he touched his high-water mark of inspiration. I have just taken it up and read it again. The conception is, to the last degree, ghostly; and it deals chiefly with that material life after death, which always had such a strong attraction for our poet.

It is the story of a woman who had been loved by three lovers—all of them now dead. One was a boy, to whom she had given but a smile's chance grace—another was Pharamond, who had died fighting in Paynim warfare. On him she had bestowed a long tress of her golden hair, which had gone with him to his grave, and grown there until its shining coils quite wrapped him round. To the third lover she had given herself; and now all these were gone,

> And all she was and all she bore
> Of rare and wonderful lay known
> To the worms only, left alone
> With faded secrets, in the core
> Of dead men's hearts.

His Life and his Work

And she began to grieve, not only for him whom she had loved, but for those others whom her love might have saved.

        Time was so bare —
    Her heart at solitary feast
    Of sorrow, sitting unreleast
Forever.

    .   .   .   .

        Oh, who would stir
    In sleep down there, and think he missed
    Aught of the faultless mouth he kissed
His life all through.

    .   .   .   .

        And since to her
    No man returned; since no more lack
Of her gave any strength to stir
    The very gravestone and come back;
And he whose soul's least word of love
Seemed a love-fetter strong enough
    To bind eternity to whole
    Eternity — since now his soul
Having content of her, or quite
    Forgetting, left her, as a thing
    Not owned, and never jealous sting
Caused him to care now, day or night,
What chance might happen to the white
    Unblemished beauty, or the heart
    His empire — ah, as houseless wraiths,
And unhoused, creeping beasts would glide
Back to a house, the day he died

Arthur O'Shaughnessy

Who cast them forth — so, from such part
Of her annulled past, full of faiths
Abjured and fruitless love and loss
   There came back to her heart the host
   Of memories comfortless; the ghost
Of every lover now might cross
   Its threshold when he would, to scare
   And grieve her with his tears, or bare
The great wound in his heart, or make
Long threat of unknown things for sake
   Of some forgotten, heedless word.

And in this solitude the thought of Pharamond — that soul of strange power, stronger
than his fate—beset her strangely, and

     The intense flower
   Of waving strange-leaved trees that sang,
   His dirge with voices wild and soft,
Wafted her perfume that had power
   To shake her heart; warm air that rang
   With ends of unknown singing, oft
Broke in upon her, as though space
   Of cold climes and cold seas between
   Were dwindling.

And yet, like the others, he came not, and
since none of these dead returned for her com-

fort, though even the spirits of those unloved in life had power to vex and haunt her, and he whom she had loved utterly lay

> Enthralled, past knowing cold or heat,
> Or hearing thunder or the feet
> Of armies —

to her, ghost-haunted and comfortless, Love came afresh—Love, who pursues our hearts forever,

> with his new
> Inconstant summer — to convert
>   And steal them from the thing they knew
> Their own — to cause them to desert
>   Their piteous memories and the few
> Fond faiths of perfect years. Alas,
> He careth not how he may hurt
>   The dead, or trouble them that wait
> In heaven, so he may bring to pass
>   Ever some new thing passionate
>   And sweet upon the earth; his sun
>   Hath need of you; and if he takes
>   Last year's spoiled roses and remakes
> Red summer with them, shall he shun
> To steal your soft hearts every one,
>   O men and women, to enrich
> His fair, new, transitory reign?

Arthur O'Shaughnessy

Thus, love-commissioned, came Chaitivel,

> Whom his fate made to love her well,
> And seek her, knowing naught of those
> That held her on the other side
> Of death.

.　　.　　.　　.　　.　　.

> A man
> Most goodly, full of all the gay
> And thrilling, summer time that rang
> Once more with rapture through the heart.

And the fair, lonesome woman's heart awakened to this summer, and blossomed anew. And he whom she had loved knew, deep in his grave, that she was false. In what she says to him, thinking of him and excusing her soul before him, and in what he answers out of his grave, there is a ghostly realism which is something unique.

> I am too distant from that shore
> Of life already,

he says, and then he cries, if that be " cry " with which the dead assail our living ears :

> Ah, haste
> To live thy false life through, that I
> May have that wrecked thing I did buy,
> A body for a soul.

His Life and his Work

But already she has cast off her bondage.
Why should she be bound, indeed, to this soul,
whose voice reaches her from the under-world,
but whose love has not been strong enough to
bring him back to save her ? She grows glad
again in the new joy of Chaitivel's wooing. But
one day a pity for Pharamond in his far-off
grave steals over her heart, and she sings a
song to his listening ghost, so subtly lovely
that it, alone, would prove its author's claim
to rank among the poets.

> Hath any loved you well, down there
>   Summer or winter through ?
> Down there have you found any fair
>   Laid in the grave with you ?
> Is death's long kiss a richer kiss
>   Than mine was wont to be,
> Or have you gone to some far bliss
>   And straight forgotten me ?
>
> What soft enamouring of sleep
>   Hath you in some soft way ?
> What charmed death holdeth you with deep,
>   Strange lure by night and day ?
> A little space below the grass
>   Out of the sun and shade,
> But worlds away from me, alas,
>   Down there where you are laid ?

Arthur O'Shaughnessy

My bright hair's waved and wasted gold,
  What is it now to thee? —
Whether the rose-red life I hold
  ‚Or white death holdeth me?
Down there you love the grave's own green,
  And ever more you rave
Of some sweet seraph you have seen
  Or dreamt of in the grave.

There you shall lie as you have lain,
  Though in the world above
Another live your life again,
  And love again your love:
Is it not sweet beneath the palm?
  Is not the warm day rife
With some long mystic golden calm
  Better than love and life?

The broad quaint odorous leaves like hands
  Weaving the fair day through
Weave sleep no burnished bird withstands
  While death weaves sleep for you;
And many a strange rich breathing sound
  Ravishes morn and noon:
And in that place you must have found
  Death a delicious swoon.

Hold me no longer for a word
  I used to say or sing:
Ah, long ago you must have heard
  So many a sweeter thing:

His Life and his Work

For rich earth must have reached your heart
And turned the faith to flowers;
And warm winds stolen, part by part
Your soul through faithless hours.

And many a soft seed must have won
Soil of some yielding thought
To bring a bloom up to the sun
That else had ne'er been brought;
And doubtless many a passionate hue
Hath made that place more fair,
Making some passionate part of you
Faithless to me down there.

And the song stole into the grave of Pharamond, and he unwound the golden tress in
whose meshes he was bound, and

. . . rose up dumb and mighty — pale
And terrible in blood-stained mail,

and went back, across lands and seas, to claim
the soul of the singer.

When her bridal day was come, then the
phantoms had their will. First of all came the
boy whose heart she had smiled away, and sat
an awesome shadow 'twixt bride and groom.

His phantom flickered as a flame
Blown blue and rent about by wind.

Arthur O'Shaughnessy

And behold,

> As they sat speechless through the day
> The spirit of the boy did stay
> Saddening them both and making cold
> Their hearts.

But when it was the bridal eve a still worse
thing befell, for he whom the lady had once
loved wholly burst his tomb, at last, and
claimed her body that had been his, and left
her faithless soul; and the soul and Chaitivel
remained together, confronting each other,
and

> She seemed an angel, thrice more fair
> Than she had seemed a woman.

Her soul would have triumphed, in this hour,
"free of the torn frame, and all acquitted,"
but then came Pharamond, and

> . . . As one might go
> Against one's death, the Chaitivel
> Went against Pharamond that night
> And met him, and the two did fight.

And so they fight on till the end.

Briefly as I have been compelled to con-
dense this Lay, I think I have given enough

of it to prove the power and originality of
its conception, and the poetic charm of its
execution.

In the other Lays are passages of great beauty;
but I have spoken in discussing this volume,
chiefly of Chaitivel, as by this poem I am
persuaded that O'Shaughnessy may be justly
judged, as to his place in the realm of imaginative narrative poetry. This volume contains,
besides the narratives, several very lovely lyrics, which will be found among the selections
that are to follow this sketch.

O'Shaughnessy's third volume was Music
and Moonlight, published in 1874—about
a year after his marriage. This volume contains not a little of its author's best work; but
it displays that fatal lack of the power of rigid
self-criticism which kept him from knowing
what not to include; and it therefore failed to
add materially to his reputation. The ode
with which it opens is so noble that, in justice
to the varied powers of this man whom, so far,
you have seen chiefly as the poet of love and
sorrow, it must be included in my selections.

One lyric from Music and Moonlight
is an especially characteristic illustration of

Arthur O'Shaughnessy

O'Shaughnessy's peculiar charm, and also of
that lack of keen self-criticism to which I have
already alluded:

> I made another garden, yea,
>   For my new love;
> I left the dead rose where it lay,
>   And set the new above.
> Why did the summer not begin?
>   Why did my heart not haste?
> My old love came and walked therein
>   And laid the garden waste.
>
> She entered with her weary smile
>   Just as of old;
> She looked around a little while,
>   And shivered at the cold.
> Her passing touch was death to all,
>   Her passing look a blight;
> She made the white rose petals fall,
>   And turned the red rose white.
>
> Her pale robe clinging to the grass
>   Seemed like a snake
> That bit the grass and ground, alas!
>   And a sad trail did make—
> She went up slowly to the gate;
>   And there, just as of yore,
> She turned back at the last to wait,
>   And say farewell once more.

His Life and his Work

This song is certainly a gem, and it might have been a flawless one but for the first half of the last stanza, which bears witness to O'Shaughnessy's lack of power to perceive defects. Every other line of the song is so perfect, that you wonder how he could have borne to say :

> Seemed like a snake
> That bit the grass and ground, alas !
> And a sad trail did make.

The subtle and half-mystical imagination of some of these poems is such as to withdraw them from popularity—from the lazy appreciation of easy-going readers; but no poet, no one, indeed, whose soul is imbued with the true love of true poetry, could read Music and Moonlight without a perception, keen even to pain, of the loss it was to the world when a pitiless winter wind blew out the brief, bright flame of this man's life.

I may not pause to speak of The Disease of the Soul—

> Oh, exquisite malady of the soul,
> How hast thou marred me !

nor yet of the Song of Betrothal, or In Love's
Eternity, much as I should like to introduce
them to the reader; but I must quote from
that poem, more audacious than almost anything even of O'Shaughnessy's, The Song of
the Holy Spirit, this fragment of description :

> The long-hushed eve
> Glowed purple, and the awed soul of the thunder
> Lay shuddering in the distance; and the heave
> Of great, unsolaced seas over and under
> The tremulous earth was heard with them to grieve.

It was a true poet who could feel the heave
of "great, unsolaced seas."

After the publication of Music and Moonlight, life was full of trouble for O'Shaughnessy. His children were born and died; his
wife, with all her wit and charm, became a
hopeless invalid, and so remained until her
death. He wanted to earn more money than
the British Museum afforded him, and he did
a good deal of prose work—papers on scien-
tific subjects, reviews, anything that could
help to fill that purse open at both ends; and
thus it chanced that he died in 1881, having
published no volume of poems since Music

and Moonlight, in 1874; and his last book—
Songs of a Worker—was given to the world
in the spring of 1881, some months after his
death.

This volume seems to me largely the tenta-
tive work of a poet in a transition state. In
the group of poems called by a singular mis-
nomer Thoughts in Marble, we certainly
find little of the cold chastity of sculpture.
The poems are, indeed, oversensuous—going
beyond even the not too rigid boundaries the
author set for himself in An Epic of Women.
The book, I must take leave to say, was too
indulgently edited by O'Shaughnessy's cousin, the Reverend Newport Deacon, who
avows, in his introduction, that of the poems
evidently intended for publication left in man-
uscript by the poet, not one has been omitted.
This too lavish inclusiveness was certainly
in some instances a grave mistake. Instead of a
well-pruned garden of choice flowers, we have
a riotous plot of blossoms, desperately sweet,
some of them, but overrun, here and there, with
weeds, and with, sometimes, more thorns than
roses. Still we can but be thankful for a volume
that gives us the Song of a Fellow Worker; a

poem so blood-red with humanity as Christ
Will Return, and, above all, anything so noble as the first part of En Soph, in which, I
think, the author approaches actual sublimity
more nearly than in any other of his poems.
We behold in it a procession of souls, passing
in review before the creating God, ere he sends
them to live, on this earth, their little lives.
In this shadowy procession the poet sees himself, and perceives, as in a vision, the pain and
passion, the long sorrow and brief joy of his
life on earth, and cries out to be spared from
it, thus :

> Oh, let me not be parted from the light !
> Oh, send me not to where the outer stars
> Tread their uncertain orbits, growing less bright
> Cycle by cycle ; where through narrowing bars
> The soul looks up and scarcely sees the throne
> It fell from ; where the stretched-out Hand,
>   that guides
> On to the end, in that dull slackening zone
> Reaches but feebly ; and where man abides
> And finds out Heaven with his heart alone.
>
> I fear to live the life that shall be mine
> Down in the half lights of that wandering world,
> 'Mid ruined angels' souls that cease to shine,
> Where fragments of the broken stars are hurled,

His Life and his Work

Quenched to the ultimate dark. Shall I believe,
  Remembering, as of some exalted dream,
The life of flame, the splendor that I leave?
  For, between life and death shall it not seem
The fond, false hope my shuddering soul would weave.

I dread the pain that I shall know on earth.
  Give me another heart, but not that one
That cannot cease to suffer from its birth
  With love, with grief, with hope; that will not shun
One human sorrow; that will pursue, indeed,
  With tears more piteous than the woes they weep,
Hearts which, soon comforted, will leave to bleed
  My heart on all the thorns of life. Oh, keep
That life from me — let me some other lead!

I fear to love as I shall love down there;
  It is not like the changeless, heavenly love.
I see a woman as an angel fair,
  And know that I shall set her face above
All other hope or memory. Day by day —
  Ah, through what agony and what despair!
My soul's eternity will melt away
  In following her. O God! I cannot bear
The passionate griefs I see along my way!

I shall not keep her; and I fear the grave
  Where she will lie at last; for though my soul
Would yearn to wreck itself, yea, even to save
  Her earthly, perishable beauty whole,

Arthur O'Shaughnessy

I shall but pray to lie down at her side
   And mingle with her dust, dreaming no dream,
Unless we wander hand in hand, or hide
   Hopeless together by some phantom stream —
Lost souls in human lives too sorely tried.

So prayed I, feeling even as I prayed
   Torments and fever of a strange unrest
Take hold upon my spirit, fain to have stayed
   In the eternal calm, and ne'er essayed
The perilous strife, the all too bitter test
   Of earthly sorrow, fearing — and ah ! too well —
To be quite ruined in some grief below,
   And ne'er regain the heaven from which I fell.
But then the angel smote my sight —'t was so
   I woke into this world of love and woe.

In this volume there are fewer of those delicate lyrics by which O'Shaughnessy is best known to his lovers than in either of the others; yet there are enough to show that the singer had not lost his power to sing. At Her Grave, written literally at his wife's grave some few months after her death, is full of pathetic charm. The Old House, Lynmouth, Eden, and half a dozen others are worthy of special mention, and I cannot refrain from allowing these two stanzas about A Rose to shed their parting fragrance over these pages:

When the Rose came I loved the Rose,
    And thought of none beside,
Forgetting all the other flowers,
    And all the others died;
And morn, and noon, and sun, and showers,
    And all things loved the Rose,
Who only half returned my love,
    Blooming alike for those.

I was the rival of a score
    Of loves on gaudy wing—
The nightingale I would implore
    For pity not to sing.
Each called her his; still I was glad
    To wait, or take my part;
I loved the Rose—who might have had
    The fairest lily's heart.

Considering the varied power displayed in this last volume, which comes to us from the dead—like a flower springing upon a grave—it moves us with more regret for the author's loss than even any of the others. He had taken to himself a new harp, but he had not yet completely strung it. His outlook was larger—

Arthur O'Shaughnessy

his sympathies were deeper. Christ Will Return was the cry of a man penetrated with the sorrows of other men, and ready to use his pen in their service. Had he lived he would have learned how to clothe his passion for humanity with the same tender grace with which in earlier days he sang the love of woman. But, literally, " a wind blew out of a cloud by night, chilling and killing " him, and, after an illness of scarcely a week's duration, the swift end came. Yet, to his thought, the cessation of this ache of living had never seemed the end. His vision pierced mysteries unknown to duller souls, and while he had so keen a sense of a life continuing underground that he could fancy his dead heart throbbing with all human pains, he yet foresaw, for that spiritual essence which was his essential self, the infinite possibilities of forever renewed life and of infinite worlds.

LOUISE CHANDLER MOULTON.

FEBRUARY, 1894.

FROM AN EPIC OF WOMEN
AND OTHER POEMS

EXILE

Des voluptés intérieures,
Le sourire mystérieux.
VICTOR HUGO.

A COMMON folk I walk among;
I speak dull things in their own tongue:
    But all the while within I hear
    A song I do not sing for fear —
How sweet, how different a thing!
    And when I come where none are near
I open all my heart and sing.

I am made one with these indeed,
And give them all the love they need —
    Such love as they would have of me:
    But in my heart — ah, let it be! —
I think of it when none is nigh —
    There is a love they shall not see;
For it I live — for it will die.

Arthur O'Shaughnessy

And ofttimes, though I share their joys,
And seem to praise them with my voice,
   Do I not celebrate my own,
   Ay, down in some far inward zone
Of thoughts in which they have no part?
   Do I not feel—ah, quite alone
With all the secret of my heart?

O when the shroud of night is spread
On these, as Death is on the dead,
   So that no sight of them shall mar
   The blessed rapture of a star —
Then I draw forth those thoughts at will;
   And like the stars those bright thoughts are;
And boundless seems the heart they fill:

For every one is as a link;
And I enchain them as I think;
   Till present and remembered bliss,
   And better worlds on after this,
I have — led on from each to each
   Athwart the limitless abyss —
In some surpassing sphere I reach.

I draw a veil across my face
Before I come back to the place

Selections from His Poems

And dull obscurity of these;
  I hide my face, and no man sees;
I learn to smile a lighter smile,
  And change and look just what they please.
It is but for a little while.

I go with them; and in their sight
I would not scorn their little light,
  Nor mock the things they hold divine;
  But when I kneel before the shrine
Of some base deity of theirs,
  I pray all inwardly to mine,
And send my soul up with my prayers:

For I — ah, to myself I say —
I have a heaven though far away;
  And there my love went long ago,
  With all the things my heart loves so;
And there my songs fly, every one:
  And I shall find them there I know
When this sad pilgrimage is done.

THE CYPRESS

O ivory bird, that shakest thy wan plumes,
    And dost forget the sweetness of thy throat
    For a most strange and melancholy note —
That will forsake the summer and the blooms
    And go to winter in a place remote!

The country where thou goest, Ivory bird!
    It hath no pleasant nesting-place for thee;
    There are no skies nor flowers fair to see,
Nor any shade at noon — as I have heard—
    But the black shadow of the Cypress tree.

The Cypress tree, it groweth on a mound;
    And sickly are the flowers it hath of May,
    Full of a false and subtle spell are they;
For whoso breathes the scent of them around,
    He shall not see the happy Summer day.

In June, it bringeth forth, O Ivory bird!
    A winter berry, bitter as the sea;
    And whoso eateth of it, woe is he —
He shall fall pale, and sleep — as I have heard—
    Long in the shadow of the Cypress tree.

A WHISPER FROM THE GRAVE

My Life points with a radiant hand
  Along a golden ray of sun
That lights some distant promised land,
  A fair way for my feet to run :
My Death stands heavily in gloom,
And digs a soft bed in the tomb
  Where I may sleep when all is done.

The flowers take hold upon my feet;
  Fair fingers beckon me along;
I find Life's promises so sweet
  Each thought within me turns to song: .
But Death stands digging for me — lest
Some day I need a little rest,
  And come to think the way too long.

O seems there not beneath each rose
  A face ? — the blush comes burning through
And eyes my heart already knows
  Are filling themselves from the blue

4*   53

Arthur O'Shaughnessy

Above the world; and One, whose hair
Holds all my sun, is coming, fair,
   And must bring heaven if all be true:

And now I have face, hair, and eyes;
   And lo, the Woman that these make
Is more than flower, and sun, and skies!
   Her slender fingers seem to take
My whole fair life, as 't were a bowl,
Wherein she pours me forth her soul,
   And bids me drink it for her sake.

Methinks the world becomes an isle;
   And there — immortal as it seems —
I gaze upon her face, whose smile
   Flows round the world in golden streams;
Ah, Death is digging for me deep,
Lest some day I should need to sleep
   And solace me with other dreams!

But now I feel as though a kiss
   Of hers should ever give me birth
In some new heaven of lifelong bliss;
   And heedlessly, athwart my mirth,
I see Death digging day by day
A grave; and, very far away,
   I hear the falling of the earth.

Selections from His Poems

Ho there, if thou wilt wait for me,
 Thou Death! — I say — keep in thy shade,
Crouch down behind the willow-tree,
 Lest thou shouldst make my love afraid.
If thou hast aught with me, pale friend,
Some flitting leaf its sigh shall lend
 To tell me when the grave is made!

And lo, e'en while I now rejoice,
 Encircled by my love's fair arm,
There cometh up to me a voice,
 Yea, through the fragrance and the charm;
Quite like some sigh the forest heaves —
Quite soft — a murmur of dead leaves,
 And not a voice that bodeth harm.

O lover, fear not — have thou joy;
 For life and love are in thy hands:
I seek in nowise to destroy
 The peace thou hast, nor make the sands
Run quicker through thy pleasant span.
Blest art thou above many a man,
 And fair is she who with thee stands.

I only keep for thee out here —
 O far away, as thou hast said,

Arthur O'Shaughnessy

Among the willow-trees — a clear,
   Soft space for slumber, and a bed ;
That, after all, if life be vain,
And love turn at the last to pain,
   Thou mayst have ease when thou art dead.

O grieve not : back to thy love's lips —
   Let her embrace thee more and more,
Consume that sweet of hers in sips ;
   I only wait till it is o'er ;
For fear thou 'lt weary of her kiss,
And come to need a bed like this
   Where none shall kiss thee evermore.

Believe each pleasant muttered vow
   She makes to thee, and see with ease
Each promised heaven before thee now :
   I only think, if one of these
Should fail thee — O thou wouldst need then
To come away, right far from men,
   And weep beneath the willow-trees.

And, therefore, have I made this place,
   Where thou shouldst come on that hard day,
Full of a sad and weary grace ;
   For here the drear wind hath its way

Selections from His Poems

With grass, and flowers, and withered tree —
As sorrow shall that day with thee,
    If it should happen as I say.

And, therefore, have I kept the ground
    As 't were quite holy, year by year.
The great wind lowers to a sound
    Of sighing as it passes near;
And seldom doth a man intrude
Upon the hallowed solitude,
    And never but to shed a tear.

So, if it be thou come, alas!
    For sake of sorrow long and deep,
I — Death, the flowers, and leaves, and grass, —
    Thy grief-fellows, do mourn and weep;
Or, if thou come, with life's whole need,
To rest a lifelong space, indeed,
    I, too, and they, do guard thy sleep.

Moreover, sometimes, while all we
    Have kept the grave with heaviness,
The weary place hath seemed to be
    Not barren of all blessedness:
Spent sunbeams rest them here at noon,
And grieving spirits from the moon
    Walk here at night in shining dress.

Arthur O'Shaughnessy

And there is gazing down on all
  Some great and love-like eye of blue
Wherefrom at times there seem to fall
  Strange looks that soothe the place quite
    through ;
As though, indeed, if all love's sweet
And all life's good should prove a cheat,
  They knew some heaven that might be true.

It is a tender voice like this
  That comes to me in accents fair :
Well, and through much of love and bliss,
  It seemeth not a thing quite bare
Of comfort, e'en to be possest
Of that one spot of earth for rest,
  Among the willow-trees down there.

BISCLAVARET

Bisclavaret ad nun en Bretan,
' Garwall l'apelent li Norman.
Jadis le poët-hum oïr,
E souvent suleit avenir,
Humes plusurs Garwall devindrent
E es boscages meisun tindrent.

MARIE DE FRANCE : LAIS.

In either mood, to bless or curse,
  God bringeth forth the breath of man;
No angel sire, no woman nurse,
  Shall change the work that God began:

One spirit shall be like a star,
  He shall delight to honor one;
Another spirit he shall mar;
  None shall undo what God hath done.

The weaker, holier season wanes;
  Night comes with darkness and with sins;
And, in all forests, hills, and plains,
  A keener, fiercer life begins.

59

Arthur O'Shaughnessy

And, sitting by the low hearth-fires,
    I start and shiver fearfully;
For thoughts all strange, and new desires
    Of distant things take hold on me;

And many a feint of touch or sound
    Assails me, and my senses leap
As in pursuit of false things found
    And lost in some dim path of sleep.

But, momently, there seems restored
    A triple strength of life and pain;
I thrill, as though a wine were poured
    Upon the pore of every vein.

I burn, as though keen wine were shed
    On all the sunken flames of sense —
Yea, till the red flame grows more red,
    And all the burning more intense,

And, sloughing weaker lives, grown wan
    With needs of sleep and weariness,
I quit the hallowed haunts of man
    And seek the mighty wilderness.

—Now over intervening waste
    Of lowland drear, and barren wold,

Selections from His Poems

I scour, and ne'er assuage my haste,
    Inflamed with yearnings manifold :

Drinking a distant sound that seems
    To come around me like a flood;
While all the track of moonlight gleams
    Before me like a streak of blood;

And bitter, stifling, scents are past
    A-dying on the night behind,
And sudden, piercing stings are cast
    Against me in the tainted wind.

And lo ! afar, the gradual stir,
    And rising of the stray wild leaves;
The swaying pine, and shivering fir,
    And windy sound that moans and heaves

In strange fits, till with utter throes
    The whole wild forest lolls about,
And all the fiercer clamor grows,
    And all the moan becomes a shout ;

And mountains near and mountains far
    Breathe freely, and the mingled roar
Is as of floods beneath some star
    Of storms, when shore cries unto shore.

Arthur O'Shaughnessy

But soon, from every hidden lair
    Beyond the forest tracks, in thick,
Wild coverts, or in deserts bare,
    Behold they come, renewed and quick,

The splendid fearful herds that stray
    By midnight, when tempestuous moons
Light them to many a shadowy prey,
    And earth beneath the thunder swoons.

O who at any time hath seen
    Sight all so fearful and so fair,
Unstricken at his heart with keen
    Whole envy at that hour to share

Their unknown curse, and all the strength
    Of the wild thirsts and lusts they know ;
The sharp joys sating them at length,
    The new and greater lusts that grow ?

But who of mortals shall rehearse
    How fair and dreadfully they stand,
Each marked with an eternal curse,
    Alien from every kin and land ?

—Along the bright and blasted heights
    Loudly their cloven footsteps ring ;

Selections from His Poems

Full on their fronts the lightning smites,
  And falls like some dazed, baffled thing.

Now through the mountain clouds they break,
  With many a crest high-antlered, reared
Athwart the storm : now they outshake
  Fierce locks or manes, glossy and weird,

That sweep with sharp perpetual sound
  The arid heights where the snows drift,
And drag the slain pines to the ground,
  And all into the whirlwind lift

The heavy sinking slopes of shade
  From hidden hills of monstrous girth,
Till the new unearthly lights have flayed
  The draping darkness from the earth.

Henceforth what hiding-place shall hide
  All hallowed spirits that in form
Of mortal stand beneath the wide
  And wandering pale eye of the storm ?

The beadsman in his lonely cell
  Hath cast one boding timorous look
Toward the heights—then loud and well,
  Kneeling before the open book,

Arthur O'Shaughnessy

All night he prayeth in one breath,
  Nor spareth now his sins to own :
And through his prayer he shuddereth
  To hear how loud the forests groan.

For all abroad the lightnings reign,
  And rally, with their lurid spell,
The multitudinous campaign
  Of hosts not yet made fast in Hell :

And us indeed no common arm,
  Nor magic of the dark, may smite ;
But through all elements of harm,
  Across the strange fields of the night,—

Enrolled with the whole giant host
  Of shadowy, cloud-outstripping things,
Whose vengeful spells are uppermost,
  And convoyed by unmeasured wings,

We foil the thin dust of fatigue
  With bright-shod phantom feet that dare
All pathless places and the league
  Of the light-shifting soils of air ;

And loud, mid fearful echoings,
  Our throats, aroused with Hell's own thirst,

Selections from His Poems

Outbay the eternal trumpetings ;
  The while, all impious and accurst,

Revealed and perfected at length
  In whole and dire transfigurement,
With miracle of growing strength
  We win upon a keen, warm scent.

Before us each cloud-fastness breaks,
  And o'er slant inward wastes of light,
And past the moving mirage-lakes,
  And on — within the Lord's own sight —

We hunt the chosen of the Lord ;
  And cease not, in wild course elate,
Until we see the flaming sword
  And Gabriel before his gate !

O many a fair and noble prey
  Falls bitterly beneath our chase ;
And no man till the judgment day
  Hath power to give these burial-place ;

But down in many a stricken home
  About the world, for these they mourn ;
And seek them yet through Christendom
  In all the lands where they were born.

Arthur O'Shaughnessy

And oft, when Hell's dread prevalence
   Is past, and once more to the earth
In chains of narrowed human sense
   We turn—around our place of birth,

We hear the new and piercing wail;
   And, through the haunted day's long glare,
In fearful lassitudes turn pale
   With thought of all the curse we bear.

But, for long seasons of the moon,
   When the whole giant earth, stretched low,
Seems straightening in a silent swoon
   Beneath the close grip of the snow,

We well nigh cheat the hideous spells
   That force our souls resistless back,
With languorous torments worse than Hell's
   To the frail body's fleshly rack;

And with our brotherhood the storms—
   Whose mighty revelry unchains
The avalanches, and deforms
   The ancient mountains and the plains—

We hold high orgies of the things,
   Strange and accursèd of all flesh,

Selections from His Poems

Whereto the quick sense ever brings
  The sharp forbidden thrill afresh.

And far away, among our kin,
  Already they account our place
With all the slain ones, and begin
  The Masses for our soul's full grace.

THE STORY OF THE KING

THIS is the story of the King:
Was he not great in everything?

He built him dwelling-places three:
In one of them his Youth should be.
    To make it fair for many a feast
    He conquered the whole East;
He brought delight from every land,
And gold from many a river's strand,
    And all things precious he could find
    In Perse, or utmost Ind.

There, brazen guarded were the doors,
And o'er the many painted floors
    The captive women came and went;
    Or, with bright ornament,
Sat in the pillared places gay,
And feasted with him every day,
    And fed him with their rosy kiss:
    O there he had all bliss!

Selections from His Poems

Then afterward, when he did hear
There was none like him anywhere,
    He would behold the sight so sweet
    Of all men at his feet;
And, since he heard that certainly
Not like a man was he to die,
    For all his lust that palace vast
    It seemed too small at last:

Therefore, another house he made,
So wide that it might hold arrayed
    The thousand peers of his domain
    And last his godlike reign.
And here he was, a goodly span,
While before came every man
    To kneel and worship in his sight:
    O there he had all might!

And yet, most surely it befel,
He tired of this house as well:
    Was it too mighty after all?
    Or still perhaps too small?
Strangely in all men's wonderment,
He left it for a tenement
    He had all builded in one year:
    Now he is dwelling there.

Arthur O'Shaughnessy

He took full little of his gold,
And of his pleasures manifold
    He had but a small heed, they say,
    That day he went away.
O, the new dwelling he hath found
Is but a man's grave in the ground,
    And taketh up but one man's space
    In the small burial-place.

And now, indeed, that he is dead,
The nations have they no more dread?
    Lo, is not this the King they swore
    To worship evermore?
Will no one Love of his come near
And kiss him while he lieth there,
    And warm his freezing lips again?—
    Is this then all his reign?

He must have longed ere this to rise
And be again in all men's eyes;
    For the place where he dwelleth now
    Lonely it is, I trow:
But, just to stand in his own hall
And feel the warmth there, once for all,
    O would he not give crowns of gold?—
    For the place is so cold!

Selections from His Poems

But over him a tomb doth stand,
The costliest in all the land ;
   And of the glory that he bore
   It telleth evermore.
So these three dwellings he hath had,
And mighty he hath been and glad :—
   O hath he not been sad as well ?
   Perhaps — but who can tell ?

   This is the story of the King :
   Was he not great in everything ?

THE FOUNTAIN OF TEARS

If you go over desert and mountain,—
    Far into the country of sorrow,—
    To-day and to-night and to-morrow,
And maybe for months and for years;
    You shall come, with a heart that is bursting
    For trouble and toiling and thirsting,
You shall certainly come to the fountain
At length,— to the Fountain of Tears.

Very peaceful the place is, and solely
    For piteous lamenting and sighing,
    And those who come living or dying
Alike from their hopes and their fears :
    Full of cypress-like shadows the place is,
    And statues that cover their faces;
But out of the gloom springs the holy
And beautiful Fountain of Tears.

And it flows and it flows with a motion
    So gentle and lovely and listless,

Selections from His Poems

And murmurs a tune so resistless
To him who hath suffered and hears,
   You shall surely — without a word spoken —
   Kneel down there and know your heart
      broken,
And yield to the long-curbed emotion
That day by the Fountain of Tears.

For it grows and it grows, as though leaping
   Up higher the more one is thinking;
   And ever its tunes go on sinking
More poignantly into the ears.
   Yea, so blessèd and good seems that fountain,
   Reached after dry desert and mountain,
You shall fall down at length in your weeping
And bathe your sad face in the tears.

Then, alas! while you lie there a season,
   And sob between living and dying,
   And give up the land you were trying
To find 'mid your hopes and your fears —
   O the world shall come up and pass o'er you,
   Strong men shall not stay to care for you,
Nor wonder indeed for what reason
Your way should seem harder than theirs.

Arthur O'Shaughnessy

But perhaps, while you lie, never lifting
    Your cheek from the wet leaves it presses,
    Nor caring to raise your wet tresses
And look how the cold world appears : —
    O perhaps the mere silences round you —
    All things in that place grief hath found you,
Yea, e'en to the clouds o'er you drifting —
May soothe you somewhat through your tears.

You may feel, when a falling leaf brushes
    Your face, as though some one had kissed you;
    Or think at least some one who missed you
Hath sent you a thought,— if that cheers;
    Or a bird's little song, faint and broken,
    May pass for a tender word spoken:
Enough, while around you there rushes
That life-drowning torrent of tears.

And the tears shall flow faster and faster,
    Brim over and baffle resistance,
    And roll down bleared roads to each distance
Of past desolation and years ;
    Till they cover the place of each sorrow,
    And leave you no Past and no Morrow:
For what man is able to master
And stem the great Fountain of Tears ?

Selections from His Poems

But the floods of the tears meet and gather ;
   The sound of them all grows as thunder :
   O into what bosom, I wonder,
Is poured the whole sorrow of years ?
   For eternity only seems keeping
   Account of the great human weeping :
May God, then, the Maker and Father —
May he find a place for the tears !

THERE IS AN EARTHLY GLIMMER
IN THE TOMB

There is an earthly glimmer in the tomb;
   And, healed in their own tears and with long
     sleep,
   My eyes unclose and feel no need to weep;
But, in the corner of the narrow room,
Behold, Love's spirit standeth, with the bloom
   That things made deathless by Death's self
     may keep.
   O what a change! for now his looks are
     deep,
And a long patient smile he can assume:
While Memory, in some soft low monotone,
   Is pouring like an oil into mine ear
   The tale of a most short and hollow bliss,
That I once throbbed, indeed, to call my own,
   Holding it hardly between joy and fear,—
   And how that broke, and how it came to
     this.

FROM LAYS OF FRANCE

.

FROM THE LAY OF THE
NIGHTINGALE

THE houses were together quite;
   The roofs and all the window places
Drew nigh, with yearning to unite;
   They were most like two lovers' faces,
Leaving just space enough for sighs,
   And fair love looks, and soft replies.
You could just see the blue above,
   You were just far enough for breath,
Indeed, just near enough for love :
   There lay a little turf beneath
Where a few sickly flowers grew,
   Chilled by the shadows of the eaves,
Warmed by the light that trembled through,
   A rose all white and with no leaves,
   Slender and like a maid that grieves,
And other blossoms, one or two.

But round about and from the sides
   At every moment you could hear
A pleasant noise of wind that glides
   Among thick boughs; for very near

Arthur O'Shaughnessy

There was a garden, and a wood
Full of sweet-scented trees that stood,
　Shivering for pleasure in the sun,
Whose shadows rustled on the wall;
　There through the day, one after one,
The sweet birds sang till even-fall;
　And then they ceased, and the night long
Sang that one sweetest of them all —
　The nightingale, O many a song,
Or all one song that could not pall,
　Of love, luxurious and long.

And heavy hazel boughs shut in
　The souls and scents of all the flowers,
　The noon, the night, and the fair hours;
And kept the place all dim within,
A pleasant place for Love's sweet sin.
　The noon fell almost to twilight
Under the heavy hazel boughs;
And the great shadow of each house
　Growing, made dark the other, quite;
There the dim time was very sweet;
　And hours between the noon and night
Were slow to pass, with lagging feet
And wings full loaded; tarried late,
　Till long fair fingers from the deep,

Selections from His Poems

Dark wood came forth to separate
  Leaves — lights from shades and love from
    sleep,—
And the moon, like a dreamed-of face
  Seen gradually in the dark,
Grew up and filled the silent place
  Between those houses wan and stark.

FROM THE LAY OF TWO LOVERS

Lady, is there indeed no place
  Beyond the world for thee and me?
 Where we may love a little space,
  And joy, as any flower or tree
That loves the sun; and half forget
  That Life our enemy hath been,
And Fate a bloodhound, keenly set
  To hunt us on, through waste and green,
And night and day, and year and year,
Lest we should hallow and make dear
  One spot of bitter earth with bliss?
Is there, indeed, beyond the day,
  Beyond the eve, beyond the sun,
  No dreamed-of place where we shall kiss,
Aye, kiss, and put all fear away,
  Death tarrying till our kiss is done? .

.   .   .   .   .

My love, I have a lay well fit
  For me to sing and thee to hear;

Selections from His Poems

For they of whom I find it writ
   Did long time, amid hope and fear,
Love secretly.

   .   .   .   .   .

They had been happy, yea, in truth
A few sweet hours of precious youth,
   Ere the world found them. Once and more
The rich effusion of some kiss
   Had warmed shy scents the roses bore,
Making the full heart of some noon
Their own most strangely in a bliss
   No summer knew or felt before
They loved ; and once and more the swoon
   Of eve had lengthened out some joy
Of theirs, delaying the hard chill
   And dim affright that would destroy
Too shortly such a day, until
   The blithe, eternal nightingale
   Had seen and known, and did not fail
To sing, that though hard fate should kill
   The twain at midnight, they had taste
Of sweet, for one rich day of life.
Many a garden place was rife
   With tender record of fond waste

Arthur O'Shaughnessy

Of hours, and broken words and sighs,
    In the long innocence when love
Kept fearful fetters on their eyes
    And lips and hearts, the more to prove
His strong life-filling flower, one day
    A bursting blossom not forborne.

But now the fair earth turned away
    Her summer from them : on no morn
Did shy beams, stealing from the sun,
    Bring early promise of joy born
To fill them till that day was done
    In some close paradise of bloom,
    Where love had made them a fair room
With unbetraying bird and tree
And sleek, scared fawn. O but to see
    The warm, bright chambers under leaf
Sun-streaked and gilded morn and noon ;
    The burrow under the arched sheaf
Whose crowned heads nodded to some tune
    Of wordless wavy motion, dim
And dense with harvest scent that drew
    The brown bee blundering o'er the rim
To drone about them, the noon through !

    .   .   .   .   .

Selections from His Poems

Their place was no more in the bloom;
All ruined was it; and their doom
  Was a thing sung of by the bird
That long had caught his rhapsody
  Straight out of their charmed thinking, heard
And felt like some· strong melody
  The corn or trees made, wordless, wild,
And wonderful; in the gray shade
The searched and trampled solitude
  Still bore the curses that defiled
Its echoes; all the mournful glade
Had heard dread shouts, and voices rude.
  Yea, the whole country no more had
One shelter of sweet green, one wood,
  One safe bright path for them, not one;
  But bitter seemed its smile, and sad,
And like an alien land it grew,
  That put scorn of them in its sun,
And death lurked in its shade, they knew.

   ·   ·   ·   ·   ·

There was no path to other lands,
  Save only by the mountain, steep
And desolate, that stood above,
  A mighty way, and seemed to sleep
On through the year, in storm or rain.

   ·   ·   ·   ·   ·

Arthur O'Shaughnessy

Fearful seemed
That mountain in the distance; slope
On slope of green they counted high
Upon its side — down which there streamed
Whole rivers fallen from the sky.
But sometimes they had even dreamed
There was a way to Heaven, past
The topmost crag and precipice.
Often a golden cloud was cast
Across it; bright, and like a piece
Of purest Heaven it floated there
And faded not: but in the fair,
Angelic moonlight a most strange
And holy smile seemed resting wide
Upon its height, working some change
Of snowy mystery: one noontide
They saw high up there, nigh the sun,
Fair arched paths, gleaming every one
As though the wingèd angels trod
Them ofttime, going up to God.

· · · · ·

So they went upward, still, to learn
The mystery of the mountain. Day
On day, they ever found some way
Higher and stranger, past return,

86

Selections from His Poems

Leading up through the solitude
They sought.

.   .   .   .   .

And never-ending sight they had
Of Heaven and higher Heaven ; and, free,
  With winged feet that were bright and glad
To walk upon the silver sea
  Of airy cloud and air, no stay
  They made, but upward the great way
  Went ever, loving ever, yea,
And drawing nigh to Love.

                    And now,
Alas, that neither I nor thou
  Can know the full and perfect fate
They have ; nor where at length they are,
  Nor for what fairer thing they wait.

.   .   .   .   .

Yet shall their fate, whate'er it be
Come very soon on me and thee !

LADIES and lovers, will ye see
How gold hair hath its perjury?
  And how the lip may twice or thrice
Undo the soul; and how the heart
  May quite annul the heart's own price
Given for many a goodly part
  Of Heaven? How one love shall be fair
  And whole and perfect in the rare,
Great likeness of an angel,— yea,
  And how another, golden-miened,
With lovely seeming and sweet way,
  Shall come and be but as a fiend
'To tempt and drag the soul away —
  And all forever? Listen well:
  This is a lay of Heaven and Hell:
Listen, and think how it shall be
With you in love's eternity.

.   .   .   .   .

This Sarrazine, of whom I sing,
Had shut her soul up from each thing

Selections from His Poems

That once with all her soul she knew
Sweet in the earth, bright in the blue;
And joyless, in the midst between
Fair blue of heaven and green earth's green,
Lived now this lovely Sarrazine,
   With passionate thinking and unknown
   Most secret flowering of her lone
And infinite beauty. All amazed
She was, and fearfully she gazed
   Into each dismal future year,
   The while it ceased not that a tear,
Born of her thought right wearily,
   Found its way backward to the drear,
Dead ashes of some memory,
   In a sweet, fatal, reckless past
   Love had made recklessly, and cast
Against her soul.
              She did not die,
But dreamed and lived, and bade the gray
Of grieving, more and more each day
Gather around and steal away
   Her hidden fairness that was bloom
   More white and wondrous in that tomb
Where the sun touched it not, and sight
Should never worship, and delight
Flower not of it, day or night.

.   .   .   .

Arthur O'Shaughnessy

Now she would weary out the days
   Joylessly looking on the white,
Slim wonder that she was, whose praise
   Henceforth must be omitted quite
Out of men's praising mouths ; whose sight
Should ne'er strike sudden with amaze
   One other heart fain to have crost
That solitude, where she must be
   Henceforth as a flower lost
Or nameless unto men.   To see
   The wild white lilies, passionless
And lonely, wasted in the rank,
Green shadowy shallows of the bank,
   Was to see many a loveliness—
No more rejected and left out,
   As a thing none cared to possess
Of love and time than, past all doubt,
   Her joyless form and face were now
Till death.   Was the world whole without
   One need of her—one thought of how
Love prospered making her—one look
   At the short, perfect miracle
His passionate hands wrought when they took
The rare, sweet elements, the fine
   And delicate fires, and wove the spell
Of her rich being ?

Selections from His Poems

Did days yet shine
And men love boundlessly and well
In the fair world beyond that cell
Of gray thoughts shutting out the sun
Her life seemed brought to ? Yea, since none
Set living heart upon her more,
And all she was, and all she bore
Of rare and wonderful lay known
To the worms only, left alone
With faded secrets in the core
Of dead men's hearts ?
Time was so bare—
Her heart at solitary feast
Of sorrow sitting unreleast
Forever !

FROM THE LAY OF ELIDUC

Now is it time, indeed, and right
   To tell of Guilliadun, the Fair.
   Sweet was her head with woven hair—
A tender color to behold,
Between the beauty of fair gold
   And some soft pallor of fair brown;
   Lovely she was, past all renown;
Her face was of no tint one knows,
Save only that of the Primrose,
   With all its strange rare seeming, too,
   That charmeth so in the spring, new
After long waiting.   Now, in truth,
All in a tender year of youth.
   She moved in her sweet maidenhood.

.   .   .   .   .

She had a sweet, bright-colored bower
Hidden with many a leaf and flower;
   Wrought all beneath the gay sunshine
   With leaf and bloom of eglantine,

Selections from His Poems

And branches green, upon the side;
There was her heart set open wide
    To heed the marvels of sweet sound,
    Of the trees singing all around.

.   .   .   .   .

God, in all things that he hath made,
Full many a jewel hath inlaid;
    For first he hath set all on high
    That fair enamel of the sky,
Brilliant of blue and eke of white;
Then he hath shed the pearl of light,
    And made that jewel-work, the seas:
    Nor less a gem, indeed, than these
I count his miracle, the Rose,
To love more precious than all those:
    But—a still fairer jewel yet—
    In every woman he hath set
Her heart; some sort of precious stone:
He shall know perfectly alone
    Who all the stars of heaven can call,
    The worth and number of them all.
Most are they given away, or sold
For so much love, or so much gold;
    Yea, no man knoweth of their cost,
    But well I ween that some are lost,

Arthur O'Shaughnessy

And some are of small worth, they say,
And some are broken, and cast away.
  It is the fairest thing you can,
    Ladies, to give this to a man—
This precious jewel that God gave:
One such is all a man may crave.

     ·   ·   ·   ·   ·

  Verily, too, Love hath some wile
Laid deeply in the sweet sunshine,
And woven in the tissue fine
  Of the mere light and floating air;
    And in the purest place his snare
Is surely set—in field, or home,
Or wheresoe'er a man may roam.

     ·   ·   ·   ·   ·

Of all the things a man may have
Before he cometh to the grave
This is the richest—to possess
One yearned-for hour in loneliness
  Beside one's love, in some fair clime,
    In some fair purple autumn time;
For quite shall be forgotten then
The pains and labors among men,
  The bitter things of doubt and fear;
    The bitter ends of hope; and, near,

Selections from His Poems

Quite at one's side, yea, on one's heart,
Yea, touching, with no more to part
   The yearning hands, or lips that meet,
   Shall seem the often dreamed-of sweet
Much more than all the glowing things
To which the fondest memory clings,
   Much more than any rapturous past,
   Or future in fair heaven at last.
And this—the fairest moment, sure,
In each man's life—it shall endure
   Some noon; while creeping twilight dims
   Slowly some flower's purple rims,
Or some green distance suffers change
Fading before us: then this strange
   And precious rapture—it shall pass,
   And never come again, alas!

FROM MUSIC AND MOONLIGHT

7

ODE

We are the music-makers,
   And we are the dreamers of dreams,
Wandering by lone sea-breakers,
   And sitting by desolate streams;
World-losers and world-forsakers,
   On whom the pale moon gleams:
Yet we are the movers and shakers
   Of the world forever, it seems.

With wonderful deathless ditties
We build up the world's great cities,
   And out of a fabulous story
   We fashion an empire's glory:
One man with a dream, at pleasure,
   Shall go forth and conquer a crown;
And three with a new song's measure
   Can trample a kingdom down.

Arthur O'Shaughnessy

We, in the ages lying
    In the buried past of the earth,
Built Nineveh with our sighing,
    And Babel itself in our mirth;
And o'erthrew them with prophesying
    To the Old of the New World's worth;
For each age is a dream that is dying,
    Or one that is coming to birth.

A breath of our inspiration
Is the life of each generation;
    A wondrous thing of our dreaming,
    Unearthly, impossible seeming—
The soldier, the king, and the peasant
    Are working together in one,
Till our dream shall become their present,
    And their work in the world be done.

They had no vision amazing
Of the goodly house they are raising;
    They had no divine foreshowing
    Of the land to which they are going:
But on one man's soul it hath broken,
    A light that doth not depart;
And his look, or a word he hath spoken,
    Wrought flame in another man's heart.

Selections from His Poems

And therefore to-day is thrilling
With a past day's late fulfilling;
   And the multitudes are enlisted
   In the faith that their fathers resisted,
And, scorning the dream of to-morrow,
   Are bringing to pass, as they may,
In the world, for its joy or its sorrow,
   The dream that was scorned yesterday.

But we, with our dreaming and singing,
   Ceaseless and sorrowless we !
The glory about us clinging
   Of the glorious futures we see,
Our souls with high music ringing :
   O men ! it must ever be
That we dwell, in our dreaming and singing,
   A little apart from ye.

For we are afar with the dawning
   And the suns that are not yet high,
And out of the infinite morning
   Intrepid you hear us cry —
How, spite of your human scorning,
   Once more God's future draws nigh,
And already goes forth the warning
   That ye of the past must die.

Arthur O'Shaughnessy

Great hail! we cry to the comers
From the dazzling unknown shore;
Bring us hither your sun and your summers,
And renew our world as of yore;
You shall teach us your song's new numbers;
And things that we dreamed not before:
Yea, in spite of a dreamer who slumbers,
And a singer who sings no more.

HAS SUMMER COME WITHOUT
THE ROSE?

Has summer come without the rose,
   Or left the bird behind?
Is the blue changed above thee,
   O world! or am I blind?
Will you change every flower that grows,
   Or only change this spot,
Where she who said, I love thee,
   Now says, I love thee not?

The skies seemed true above thee,
   The rose true on the tree;
The birds seemed true the summer through,
   But all proved false to me.
World, is there one good thing in you,
   Life, love, or death — or what?
Since lips that sang, I love thee,
   Have said, I love thee not?

Arthur O'Shaughnessy

I think the sun's kiss will scarce fall
    Into one flower's gold cup;
I think the bird will miss me,
    And give the summer up.
O sweet place! desolate in tall,
    Wild grass, have you forgot
How her lips loved to kiss me,
    Now that they kiss me not?

Be false or fair above me,
    Come back with any face,
Summer! — do I care what you do?
    You cannot change one place —
The grass, the leaves, the earth, the dew,
    The grave I make the spot —
Here, where she used to love me,
    Here, where she loves me not.

THREE GIFTS

Love took three gifts and came to greet
  My heart. Love gave me what he had,
The first thing sweet, the second sweet,
  And the last thing sweet and sad.

The first thing was a lily wan,
  The second was a rose full red,
The third thing was my lady-swan,
  My lady-love lying dead.

Come and kiss us, come and see
  How Love hath wrought with her and me;
Over our grave the years shall creep,
  Under the years we two shall sleep.

NOW I AM ON THE EARTH

Now I am on the earth,
  What sweet things love me?
Summer, that gave me birth,
  And glows on still above me;
The bird I loved a little while;
  The rose I planted;
The woman in whose golden smile
  Life seems enchanted.

Now I am in the grave,
  What sweet things mourn me?
Summer, that all joys gave,
  Whence death, alas! hath torn me;
One bird that sang to me; one rose
  Whose beauty moved me;
One changeless woman; yea, all those
  That living loved me.

A DREAM

A Dream took hold of the heart of a man,
To hold it more than a mere dream can;
For the Dream was wonderful, glorious, bright,
A splendor by day and a love by night,
In an earth all heaven, in a heaven all light—
For the Dream was a woman, womanly, white.

And the Dream became such a part of the man,
That it did for him more than a mere dream can;
For soothing sorrows, transforming tears,
It lifted him higher than hopes and fears;
It dwelt with him days, and months, and years,—
Was love and religion, and faith and prayers.

And who need be told how that Dream began
To fail and to fade from the heart of the man?
Nay, it vanished, it broke, as the fitfullest gleam
Of the sun that fades on the fitfullest stream;
And there went with it love and religion, I deem,
And faith, and glory, and hope, it would seem;
For that Dream was a Woman, that Woman
    a Dream.

AT THE LAST

By weary paths and wide
Up many a torn hillside,
Through all the raging strife
And the wandering of life,
Here on the mountain's brow
I find, I know not how,
My long-neglected shrine
Still holy and still mine.

The wall, with leaves o'ergrown,
Is ruined, not o'erthrown;
Surely the door hath been
Guarded by one unseen;
Surely the prayer last prayed
And the dream last dreamed have stayed.
I will enter, and try once more
To dream and pray as of yore.

FROM SONGS OF A WORKER

AT HER GRAVE

I HAVE stayed too long from your grave, it seems;
   Now I come back again;
Love, have you stirred down there in your dreams
   Through the sunny days or the rain?
Ah, no! the same peace; you are happy so;
And your flowers, how do they grow?

Your rose has a bud: is it meant for me?
   Ah, little red gift put up
So silently, like a child's present, you see
   Lying beside your cup!
And geranium-leaves — I will take if I may,
Two or three to carry away.

I went not far. In yon world of ours
   Grow ugly weeds. With my heart,
Thinking of you and your garden of flowers,
   I went to do my part;
Plucking up where they poison the human wheat
The weeds of cant and deceit.

Arthur O'Shaughnessy

'T is a hideous thing I have seen, and the toil
    Begets few thanks, much hate;
And the new crop only will find the soil
    Less foul; for the old 't is too late.
I come back to the only spot I know
Where a weed will never grow.

LYNMOUTH

I HAVE brought her I love to this sweet place,
    Far away from the world of men and strife,
That I may talk to her a charmèd space,
    And make a long, rich memory in my life.

Around my love and me the brooding hills,
    Full of delicious murmurs, rise on high,
Closing upon this spot the summer fills,
    And over which there rules the summer sky.

Behind us on the shore down there, the sea
    Roars roughly, like a fierce pursuing hound;
But all this hour is calm for her and me;
    And now another hill shuts out the sound.

And now we breathe the odors of the glen,
    And round about us are enchanted things;
The bird that hath blithe speech unknown to
        men,
    The river keen, that hath a voice and sings.

Arthur O'Shaughnessy

The tree that dwells with one ecstatic thought,
　　Wider and fairer growing year by year;
The flower that flowereth and knoweth naught;
　　The bee that scents the flower and draweth
　　　　near.

Our path is here, the rocky winding ledge
　　That sheer o'erhangs the rapid shouting
　　　　stream
Now dips down smoothly to the quiet edge,
　　Where restful waters lie as in a dream.

The green exuberant branches overhead
　　Sport with the golden magic of the sun,
Here quite shut out, here like rare jewels shed
　　To fright the glittering lizards as they run.

And wonderful are all those mossy floors
　　Spread out beneath us in some pathless place,
Where the sun only reaches and outpours
　　His smile, where never foot hath left a trace.

And there are perfect nooks that have been
　　　　made
　　By the long-growing tree, through some
　　　　chance turn

Its trunk took; since transformed with scent
    and shade,
  And filled with all the glory of the fern.

And tender-tinted wood flowers are seen,
  Clear starry blooms, and bells of pensive blue,
That lead their delicate lives there in the green —
  What were the world if it should lose their
    hue?

Even o'er the rough out-jutting stone that blocks
  The narrow way some cunning hand hath
    strewn
The moss in rich adornment, and the rocks
  Down there seem written thick with many
    a rune.

And here, upon that stone, we rest awhile,
  For we can see the lovely river's fall,
And wild and sweet the place is to beguile
  My love, and keep her till I tell her all.

The thing I have to tell her is so great,
  The words themselves would seem of little
    worth;
But here grand voices at my bidding wait,
  The torrent is my heart, and roars it forth.

Arthur O'Shaughnessy

I take my love's hand; looking in her eyes,
   I strive to speak, but the thought grows too
     vast —
Lo! a bird helps me out with it; she sighs;
   Sing on, sweet bird, 't will reach her heart
     at last!

Oh, torrent, say thou art this heart of mine,
   Strong, rapid, overwhelming; I will break
Life's very rocks with rage akin to thine,
   And conquer, ever striving for her sake.

Oh, bird, sing thou art even the voice my heart
   Will find to woo her life through, day by day,
So that she hearing never shall depart,
   And the long way shall seem a little way.

Oh, wandering river that my love and I
   Behold to-day through many a leafy screen,
Tell her that life shall be a gliding by
   A course like thine through this enchanted
     scene.

A LOVE SYMPHONY

Along the garden ways just now
  I heard the flowers speak;
The white rose told me of your brow,
  The red rose of your cheek.
The lily of your bended head,
  The bindweed of your hair :
Each looked its loveliest and said
  You were more fair.

I went into the wood anon,
  And heard the wild birds sing,
How sweet you were ; they warbled on,
  Piped, trilled the selfsame thing.
Thrush, blackbird, linnet, without pause,
  The burden did repeat,
And still began again because
  You were more sweet.

And then I went down to the sea,
  And heard it murmuring too,

Arthur O'Shaughnessy

Part of an ancient mystery,
   All made of me and you.
How many a thousand years ago
   I loved, and you were sweet,
Longer I could not stay, and so,
   I fled back to your feet.

IN A BOWER

A PATH led hither from the house
  Where I have left your doubt and pain,
    O fettered days of all my past;
    I lingered long, but came at last;
One lifting up of fragrant boughs,
  Then love was here and broke my chain
    With eager hands: the die is cast,
No path leads back again.

Henceforth, cold tyrant of my heart,
  You rule no longer pulse or breath;
    Love, with rich words and kisses hot
    Has told me truth in this charmed spot;
And, though your hand this hour should part
  The leaves, I have no thought, but saith
    My life is Love's: I fear you not,
Now you are only Death.

And Death creeps up the garden walk;
  But Love hastes, winning more and more:

Arthur O'Shaughnessy

My hands, my mouth are his, my hair,
My breast, as all my first thoughts were ;
Across the moonlit sward Death stalks ;
But Love upon this flower-strewn floor
Hath made me wholly his : ah, there !
Death stands outside the door.

.